Little Stories for Funtime

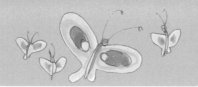

A catalogue record for this book is available from the British Library

Published by Ladybird Books Ltd
27 Wrights Lane London W8 5TZ
A Penguin Company
© LADYBIRD BOOKS LTD MCMXCIX

Stories in this book were previously published by Ladybird Books Ltd
in the *Little Stories* series.

LADYBIRD and the device of a Ladybird are trademarks of Ladybird Books Ltd

Little Stories for Funtime

Ladybird

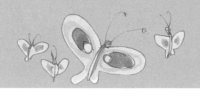

Introduction

This collection of Little Stories was written with special little people in mind.

Each of the little characters in this book is faced with a big problem. But each of them soon shows that being little doesn't mean you can't be brave or bold, clever or kind...

Contents

Bold Little Tiger
by Joan Stimson
illustrated by Jan Lewis

Little Lost Puppy
by Ronne Randall
illustrated by Karen Hiscock

Big Little Bus
by Nicola Baxter
illustrated by Toni Goffe

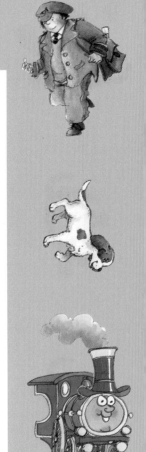

Brave Little Train
by Nicola Baxter
illustrated by Toni Goffe

Busy Little Postman
by Karen King
illustrated by Harmen van Straaten

Bold
Little
Tiger

Each morning, when he woke
up, Little Tiger always said the
same thing:

*"I'm tall and I'm tough.
I'm growly and gruff."*

And then he prowled proudly
round his Big Sisters on tiptoe.

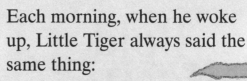

Good morning,
Big Sisters!

But Little Tiger's Big Sisters didn't take him seriously.

"You're not grown-up enough to come with us," they told him.

So one day, Little Tiger set off on an adventure… all on his own.

Not far from home was a steep bank.

"WHEEEEEE!" Little Tiger was just whizzing down it for the tenth time, when he heard a cry for help.

Instantly, Little Tiger was on the alert.

Watch your paws, Little Tiger!

Wheee

"*I'm tall and I'm tough.
I'm growly and gruff,*"
he called. Then he picked himself
up and leapt off to investigate.

Help!

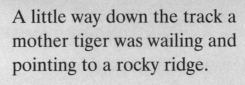

A little way down the track a mother tiger was wailing and pointing to a rocky ridge.

"My cubs are stranded," she groaned. "I only turned my back for two minutes and they crept off… along that narrow ledge."

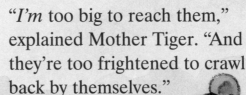

"*I'm* too big to reach them," explained Mother Tiger. "And they're too frightened to crawl back by themselves."

Little Tiger drew himself up to his full height and looked bold.

"I'm tall and I'm tough.
I'm growly and gruff…"

he told Mother Tiger. "And I'm exactly the right size to rescue your cubs."

We didn't mean to come this far!

Little Tiger bounded towards the rocky ridge.

"Just wait till I tell my Big Sisters about *this*," he thought to himself.

Before long, he was able to leap onto the narrow ledge where the cubs were huddled together.

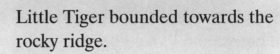

*"I'm tall and I'm tough.
I'm growly and gruff…"*
bellowed Little Tiger, "And here
I am to make one of my daring
high ridge rescues."

This is easy!

Little Tiger waited for the cubs to tell him how brave he was. But to his horror, they scuttled backwards… towards the edge of the ridge.

"Don't shout!" they whimpered. "We're scared and we want our mum."

"Oh, no," groaned Little Tiger. "These cubs are so frightened that I'm going to have to WHISPER. And I haven't done that since I was a cub myself."

Little Tiger looked nervously over his shoulder.

"Thank goodness my Big Sisters can't hear me," he told himself.

And at last he managed a whispery hiss.

"I'm a friend," he explained to the cubs. "And I've come to help you."

We want a story first!

To Little Tiger's relief, the cubs
stopped scuttling backwards. But
then they refused to climb onto
his back.

"We want a story first," they
announced. "Mum always tells us
a story when we've had a shock."

Oh, no!

"A STORY!" bellowed Little Tiger.
"I'm tall and I'm tough.
I'm growly and gruff…
and I didn't crawl along this
dangerous ledge to tell stories!"

But when the cubs leapt backwards
again, Little Tiger was forced to
think quickly. Once more he looked
nervously over his shoulder.
"At least my Big Sisters can't see
me," said Little Tiger.

Don't be
frightened
of him.

And then he began, "Once upon a time there were two tiny tigers…"

"Oooh!" squealed the cubs, "that sounds exciting." And they listened eagerly as Little Tiger told the tale of two small cubs who had to be rescued… by the bravest and boldest tiger in the jungle.

At last the cubs clambered onto Little Tiger's back.

They're happy now!

This is fun!

"Hold tight," he told them. "And look straight ahead to where your mum is waiting."

At the word 'mum' the cubs began to whimper again.

"We want our mum," they sniffed. "We want her to hug us and to sing *The Little Jungle Jingle*." But then they had a bright idea.

"You can sing *The Little Jungle Jingle* with us," they told Little Tiger. "And then we won't be frightened."

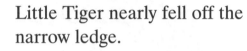

Little Tiger nearly fell off the narrow ledge.

"THE LITTLE JUNGLE JINGLE!" he hissed. "I don't know the words to any Jungle Jingle."

"We do!" chorused the cubs. And as soon as he'd checked that his Big Sisters were still out of sight, Little Tiger was forced to sing…

> Jungle cubs, jungle cubs,
> Jog along the track.
> Fur, paws and BUMPSY cubs!
> It's time we all jogged back.

By the time he'd wriggled and sung his way to the end of the ledge, Little Tiger was *EXHAUSTED*!

But Mother Tiger was beaming
with relief. And Little Tiger's
Big Sisters had arrived to see
what all the noise was about.

"Listen to us," shrieked the cubs.
"And listen to Little Tiger join in."

"OH, NO!" shuddered Little Tiger.
"I'm going to have to sing *The Little
Jungle Jingle* again. And this time
my Big Sisters will hear me."

We won't
climb so high
next time!

But Little Tiger was in for a
surprise. Because, by now, the cubs
were prowling round their mum on
tiptoe and growling,

"I'm tall and I'm tough.
I'm growly and gruff…
and, when we grow up," they
announced, "we want to be as
brave and as bold as Little Tiger!"

"Of course you do," said Mother Tiger. "Anyone can see that Little Tiger is a very bold tiger indeed. And I couldn't have managed without him."

Little Tiger's Big Sisters looked at each other in amazement. Then they took a long look at their brother.

"Come on, Little Tiger," they both cried at once. "It's time you joined in with *us*!"

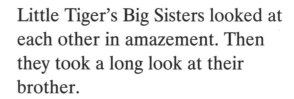

We're tall and we're tough. We're growly and gruff, and we all ROAR together!

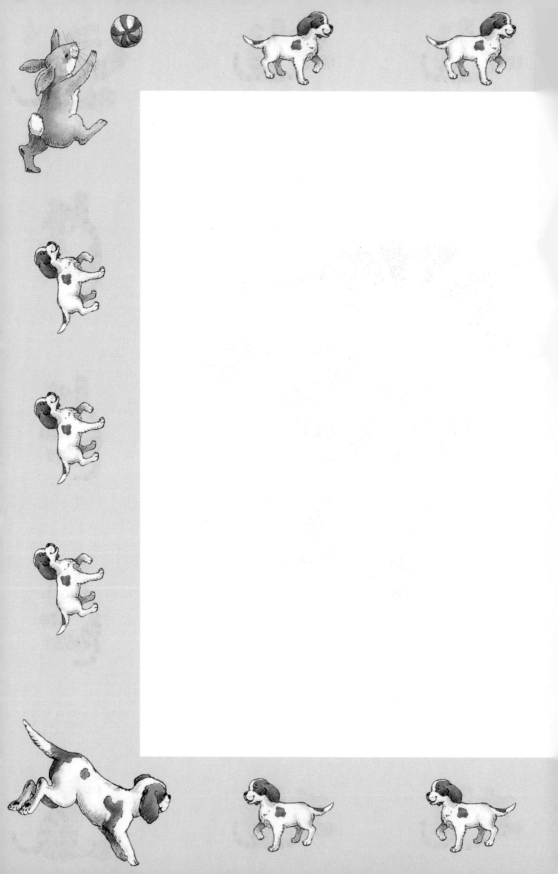

Little
Lost Puppy

Little Puppy and Bunny were best friends.

Every day they played tag, and chase-the-ball, and who-can-jump-higher, and hide-and-seek.

They had so much fun together!

Then one day Bunny moved away to a new home.

Little Puppy was sad and missed his friend. But then he realised that he could visit Bunny, and they could play together as they always did.

Bunny's new home was far away.
So Little Puppy made up a special
rhyme to help him remember how
to get there:

"Down the lane
And past the mill,
Turn right at the big tree
Over the hill…

> *Past the field
> Where the horses play –
> I'm off to see Bunny
> And I know the way!"*

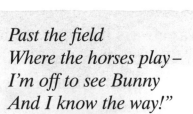

Where are you going, Little Puppy?

I'm off to see my friend, Bunny!

Bunny was always happy to see his friend. And Little Puppy was happy to be there. But sometimes he felt just a little worried.

"What if I forget the way next time I come?" he asked Bunny. "Or what if I get lost going home?"

"You don't need to worry," Bunny told him. "If you get lost, just go back the way you came! All you have to do is to think of this rhyme:

"If you lose your way,
Don't be downhearted –
Just follow your steps
Back to where you started!"

One night, there was a loud and blustery storm. The wind howled and moaned and shook the branches of the trees. Little Puppy couldn't sleep.

"I hope I'll be able to visit Bunny tomorrow," he thought.

I can't sleep in this storm.

By next morning the storm was over. The air was calm and clear, and the sun was shining.

"I *will* be able to visit Bunny today," thought Little Puppy happily.

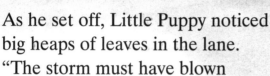

As he set off, Little Puppy noticed
big heaps of leaves in the lane.
"The storm must have blown
them from the trees last night,"
he thought.

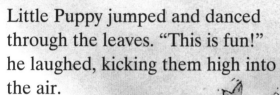

Little Puppy jumped and danced
through the leaves. "This is fun!"
he laughed, kicking them high into
the air.

As he went along, Little Puppy said his rhyme to himself:

> *"Down the lane*
> *And past the mill,*
> *Turn right at the big tree*
> *Over the hill!"*

Where's the big tree?

He clambered happily over the hill
as he always did, and scurried down
the other side.

Suddenly Little Puppy stopped.
Where was the big tree? He
couldn't see it anywhere!

Little Puppy was so confused that he didn't know which way to turn. He ran down the lane, trying to remember the rest of the way to Bunny's house.

"Past the field where the horses play," he said to himself. *"That is the way to Bunny's today!"*

But Little Puppy didn't see the field where the friendly horses played. Instead he saw a mossy stone wall and an old barn.

"I can't remember seeing *this* on the way to Bunny's house," he thought as he passed by.

Little Puppy went on, and after a while he did come to a field.

"*This* must be where the horses play!" he said to himself. But it wasn't. There were no horses in this field, just a raggedy old scarecrow.

"I can't remember seeing *this* on the way to Bunny's house!" said Little Puppy. He was *very* worried now. In fact, he felt like crying.

Then Little Puppy remembered
what Bunny had told him:

> *'If you lose your way,*
> *don't be downhearted –*
> *Just follow your steps*
> *Back to where you started!'*

"*That's* what I need to do," thought
Little Puppy. "I'll go back the way
I came!"

Back Little Puppy went,
past the scarecrow…
past the old barn…
and past the mossy wall.

At last Little Puppy found himself
back at the bottom of the hill.

"I know where I am now," he said
happily. "And there's the big tree.
It must have blown over in the storm
last night!"

Little Puppy leapt over the tree trunk, and scampered merrily down the lane. Before he knew it he could see his friends the horses.

"*Here's* the field where the horses play," he said. "*This* is the way to Bunny's today!"

There you are, Little Puppy!

We missed you!

And so Little Puppy found his way
to Bunny's home at last.

"Oh, I'm so glad to see you!"
Bunny exclaimed. "I was worried –
I thought you might have got lost!"

"I did get lost," said Little Puppy.

"Then how did you get here?"
asked Bunny.

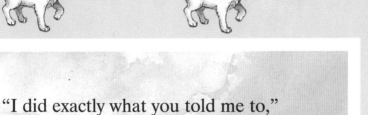

"I did exactly what you told me to," said Little Puppy. "Although I was lost, I wasn't downhearted – I just followed my steps back to where I started!"

"You went back the way you came!" said Bunny.

"Yes," said Little Puppy. "And now that I know how to do that, I'll never worry about getting lost again!"

And off they went for a lively game of tag.

Big
Little
Bus

"BOOP! BOOP! Move over, Little Bus," boomed the Big Bus, rumbling out of the garage.

"Oooh nooo," tooted the Little Bus, "I've got to go! There'll be lots of passengers for the Grand Pet Show!"

"Lots!" laughed the Big Bus. "But you're so LITTLE! You can't carry *lots* of anything!"

The Little Bus chugged off down
the road, feeling smaller than ever.

At the first bus stop, a *very* tired lady was waiting. But she was not alone. She had a baby in a buggy, and a puppy (called Pickle), and six *enormous* bags of shopping.

"Is there room for us?" she called.

"Well…," sighed the Little Bus. "I'm not a very *big* bus. But I'll try."

So the lady with the baby climbed on board.

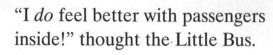

"I *do* feel better with passengers inside!" thought the Little Bus.

But as she trundled along…

…the puppy started to wriggle

…the shopping bags started to jiggle

…and the baby started to cry.

Soon there were bottles and tins and baby things all *over* the bus.

What a TERRIBLE mess!

At the next stop was a man in a suit.

"Can I get a seat with my parrot called Pete?" he asked.

The Little Bus sighed. "I'm quite full already, but climb up and see!"

I feel wobbly on my wheels!

So the man got on the bus. He picked up the bottles and tins and baby things. He smiled at the lady and made faces at the baby.

The parrot called Pete hopped up on the seat. Pete wiggled, the baby giggled and Pickle sat still at last.

Big birdie!

At the next stop, there were two more passengers.

"Can you squeeze us in?" called a lady in a hat with a very fat cat.

"I'm not very big," called the Little Bus, "but there's room for two!"

The lady in the hat bustled to the back. The man in a suit tried to pat the fat cat.

"Puss Puss Purrfect is rather shy," said her owner, with a sigh.

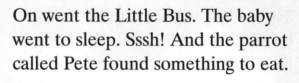

On went the Little Bus. The baby went to sleep. Sssh! And the parrot called Pete found something to eat.

At the next bus stop, three little girls stood in a row.

They called, "Can you take us to the Grand Pet Show?"

"Yes! Jump on board… all of you!" said the Little Bus.

For each little girl had two white
mice, who scampered and skipped
and twizzled their tails.

At the next bus stop there was one small boy.

"Is there room for me?" he called.

"Well…," said the Little Bus.

But the lady in the hat called out, "What's in that box? Will it upset Puss Puss Purrfect?"

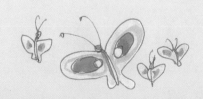

And the little girls cried, "Does it eat pets that scamper and skip?"

And everyone else whispered, "*Ssshhhh!* Will it wake the baby?"

And they all got off the bus to have a look.

It isn't a tiger!

The little boy held his box proudly. "In here," he said, "are exactly one hundred and twenty-four crawly caterpillars. They're *very* quiet and they *cannot* escape!"

"My baby is very crawly and he *often* tries to escape!" said the lady.

But the box *was* tied up well, and the little boy got on the bus.

So the lady with the baby and the buggy and the puppy (called Pickle)…

the man in a suit with a parrot (called Pete)…

the lady in a hat with a very fat cat…

the three little girls with their six white mice…

and the boy with a box of one hundred and twenty-four crawly caterpillars…

and the Little Bus set off…

GRAND PET SHOW THIS WAY

for the Grand Pet Show.

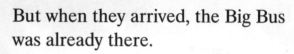

But when they arrived, the Big Bus
was already there.

"BOOP! BOOP!" he boomed.
"I've brought sixty-six passengers
all the way here."

"Only *sixty-six*?" tooted the Little
Bus. "*I've* done better than that!
But I'm not very good at counting."

Oh no,
not him again!

"I am! I counted *all* my caterpillars.
Now…" said the little boy,

"The lady and her baby make one and two… and the puppy (called Pickle) makes three.

Four and five are the man in a suit and his parrot (called Pete)…

the lady in the hat and her very fat cat make six and seven… *but* the cat isn't fat! She's had four kittens! Eight, nine, ten, eleven!

The three little girls and their six white mice add up to… twenty!

I'm twenty-one," said the boy,
undoing his box, "and here are
exactly one hundred and
twenty-four...

beautiful BUTTERFLIES!"

The passengers cheered and the baby chuckled.

The puppy barked and the parrot squawked.

And while the butterflies fluttered
high overhead, everyone waved
goodbye and said,

"You're the

BIGGEST

Little Bus in the world!"

I'm a star!

Brave
Little
Train

Pht! Pht! Pht! Pht! Phoooooh!

The Station Master shook his head. "I'm sorry," he said. "The Seaside Express simply will not start."

"Oh nooo!" wailed the passengers on the platform, waving their tickets.

"No sandcastles!" cried a boy with four big buckets.

"No paddling!" groaned a businessman with a bushy beard.

"No ice cream!" sniffed the twins.

"NO PROBLEM! The Little Train will make the trip instead!" called the Station Master.

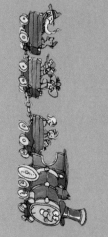

That Little Train will never make it.

"I know this is your first long trip," he said, "but remember, all you have to do is follow the track."

"But, but, but… it's a very long way!" spluttered the Little Train.

"You can do it!" said the Station Master, picking up his whistle.

Whooooooooo! went the whistle.

"Hooraaaaaaaay!" called the passengers.

"Oh… oh… oh… well… here we g-g-go!" puffed the Little Train, and slowly he pulled his three crowded carriages out of the station.

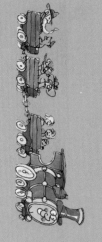

But I'm only a little train!

As soon as he was on the open track, the Little Train felt better.

"This, this, this… isn't so bad!" he chuffed quietly to himself.

"We're going to the sea!" yelled the terrible twins.

"It's a very smooth ride!" smiled the lady in blue.

"It's a first class train!" said the businessman with the beard.

"It's fine, fine, fine – if there aren't any hills!" puttered the Little Train under his breath.

But two minutes later…

There goes the Little Train!

So far, so good.

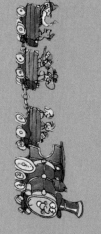
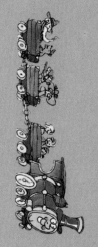

"Ooooooooo…er!" yelled the passengers, as they started to climb.

"Help! There goes my hat!" cried the lady in blue.

"Allow me, Madam!" called the businessman with the beard.

"We've caught it with our spades!" screamed the twins together.

"Uphill isn't s-s-so bad – if there isn't any downhill!" puffed the Little Train, red in the face.

But when he got to the top…

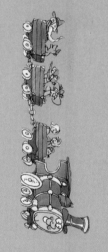

"Wheeeeeeeeeeee!" screeched the passengers.

"It's just like the fair!" shouted the boy with the buckets.

"This could blow my beard off!" moaned the man with the whiskers.

"It's almost fun – as long as there are no bridges!" squealed the Little Train as the wind whistled through his wheels.

But just around the corner…

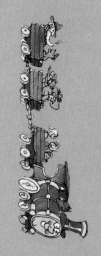

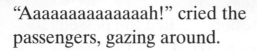

"Aaaaaaaaaaaaaah!" cried the passengers, gazing around.

"Look at the view!" cried the lady in blue.

"It's a long, long way down!" called the boy with the buckets.

"Don't lean out!" yelled his mother and father.

"I just can't look…" worried the Little Train as he rattled over the bridge.

And when he did open his eyes…

"Ooooooh!" called the passengers as they whizzed into the tunnel.

"Ooooooh!" echoed the tunnel as the Little Train rushed through.

It's dark!

It's the darkest dark I've ever seen!

It's very dark!

"Woooooooooooooh!" whistled the brave Little Train. "I'm, I'm, I'm… going to get through!"

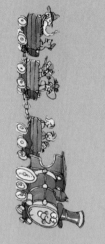

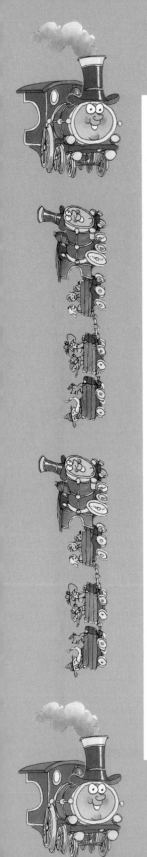

And in just a few minutes, they were all safely through the tunnel.

"Phewwwwwww!" yelled the passengers, looking around.

"Where are my sunglasses?" cried the lady in blue.

"I've dropped my ticket!" shouted the boy with the buckets.

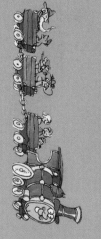

"Oh no, not again!" groaned his mother and father.

"I'm, I'm, I'm… beginning to like this!" chuffed the cheerful Little Train.

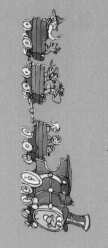

But ahead on the line stood
something large and lazy.

"Hold on to your seats everyone!"
shrieked the Little Train.

"Shooooo!" cried the passengers.

"Moooooo!" said the cow as the
Little Train rushed towards her.

"Get off the line!" barked the man
with the beard.

"I, I, I… can't s-s-s-stop!" screeched the Little Train, braking as hard as any train could.

Silly moo!

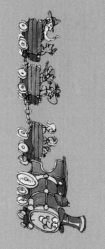

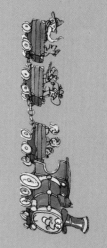

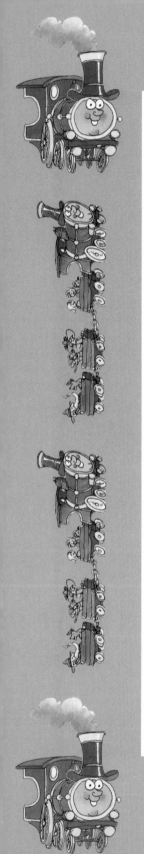

But just as it seemed that disaster was near, the cow leapt away and at last the track was clear.

"Hooooooooraaaaaaaay!" called the passengers, chuckling and cheering.

"Phew, phew, phew, phew… is
there much farther to go?" sighed
the Little Train, beginning to run
out of steam.

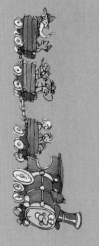

Are we
nearly there?

I'm going
to write to
the farmer!

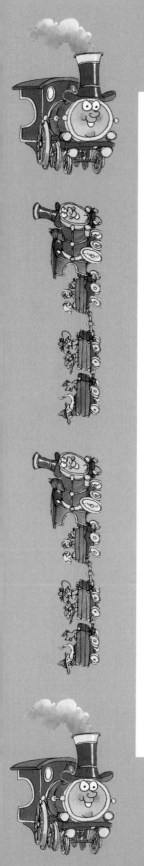

But round the next bend was the end of the line!

"The seeeeeeeeeea!" cheered the passengers, smiling and waving.

Don't you dare land on my hat!

"Nearly, nearly, nearly… there,"
sighed the tired Little Train, as the
passengers jostled and jiggled and
giggled on their way to the sea.

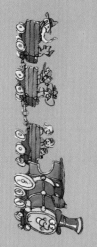

"Goodbyeeeeeeeeeee!" called the passengers, leaving the station.

"We'll see you later!" called the terrible twins, swinging their spades in a dangerous way!

"What time do we leave?" laughed the lady in blue.

"At six o'clock sharp," said the smart Station Mistress. "You'll be rested by then, won't you, Little Train?"

"Yes!" The brave Little Train gave
a sigh and a smile. And happily
dreaming of making great journeys,
he soon fell asleep to the sounds of
the sea.

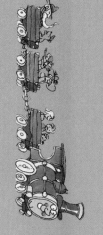

Double ice
creams first!

Busy
Little
Postman

The Little Postman was in a rush.
He had lots of mail to deliver.
There was a big sack of letters. And
a Very Big Parcel. On the front of
the parcel, in big letters, was
written HAPPY BIRTHDAY.

"Goodness, what a Very Big
Parcel," said the Little Postman.
"I wonder whose birthday present
it is?"

As he picked up the Very Big
Parcel he didn't notice a label fall
onto the floor.

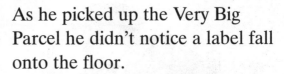

"Dearie me, there's no name or address written on it," sighed the Little Postman. "How will I know who to deliver it to?"

Then he had an idea. "I'll ask everyone if it's their birthday today and then I'll know who the parcel is for," he decided.

So the Little Postman put the big sack of letters and the Very Big Parcel in the back of his van and set off to deliver them.

First stop was Rose Cottage where Mary Moore, the carpenter, lived.

He sorted out Mary's letters, walked up the garden path, and rang the chimes on Mary's bright blue door.

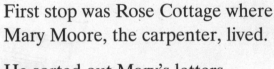

"Hello, Mary," said the Little Postman, giving her a big grey envelope and a postcard from Africa with a yellow stamp on it. "Is it your birthday today?"

Rose cottage

Phew! This is heavy!

"Goodness, no. My birthday was last month," Mary told him.

"Then this parcel isn't for you," said the Little Postman, and he carried the Very Big Parcel back to his van.

Wait a minute!

"Wait a minute…!" shouted Mary, and ran after him. But the Little Postman was already driving off.

The Little Postman drove down the road and round the corner. He pulled up outside John Jones, the tailor's, house.

"Hello, John," said the Little Postman, giving him two letters with green stamps on them. "Is it your birthday today?"

"No, it's ages yet," said John.

"Then this parcel isn't for you," said the Little Postman, and he carried the Very Big Parcel back to his van.

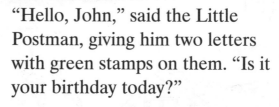

"Hey, hang on…!" shouted John and ran outside. But the Little Postman was already driving off.

JOHN JONES
tailor

It isn't my birthday.

JOHN JON
tailor

Next stop was Lucy Love, the artist's, house.

"Hello, Lucy," said the Little Postman, giving her a small packet. "Is it your birthday today?"

"No, it's next month," said Lucy.

"Then this parcel isn't for you," said the Little Postman, and he carried the Very Big Parcel back to his van.

"Come back…!" shouted Lucy, and ran outside. But the Little Postman was already driving off.

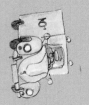

Then he drove up another hill, down a lane, and stopped outside number 334 where Granny Green lived.

He had to ring the bell three times and shout through the letter box before Granny Green opened the door.

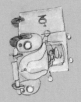

"Sorry, I was icing a cake," said Granny.

The Little Postman gave her a blue airmail letter from America.

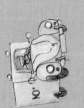

"Is it your birthday today?" he asked.

"No," said Granny. "My birthday is in the winter."

"Then this parcel isn't for you," said the Little Postman, and he carried the Very Big Parcel back to his van.

"Wait a minute…!" said Granny,
and she ran to the door. But the
Little Postman had driven away.

It's from my son!

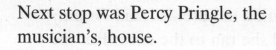

Next stop was Percy Pringle, the musician's, house.

"Is it your birthday today?" asked the Little Postman, giving Percy a letter.

"No, it's months away," said Percy.

"Well, I've almost finished delivering my letters, and I still don't know whose parcel this is," sighed the Little Postman. "If I can't find out, I'll have to take it back to the Post Office."

And he carried the Very Big Parcel back to his van.

"Hey, stop…!" shouted Percy, and ran outside. But the Little Postman was already driving off to deliver his last few letters.

I know whose parcel it is!

Percy quickly phoned Mary Moore,
and Mary Moore phoned John
Jones, and John Jones phoned
Lucy Love and Lucy Love
phoned Granny Green.

"He'll soon be on his way back
to the Post Office," Percy said.

The Little Postman drove all the
way back to the Post Office. Then,
he took the Very Big Parcel out of
the back of the van.

"Now, how *can* I find out whose parcel this is?" he thought as he carried it back into the Post Office…

There were Mary Moore and John Jones and Lucy Love and Granny Green and Percy Pringle all waiting for him.

"*HAPPY BIRTHDAY!*" they all shouted.

"Thank you," smiled the Little Postman. "I forgot it was my birthday today."

"We didn't," said Granny Green. "I've made you this cake."

"And this is *your* present," said John Jones. "The label fell off, look!"

Then Percy Pringle led the singing –

Happy Birthday to you.
Happy Birthday to you.
Happy Birthday, Little Postman.
Happy Birthday to you!

The Little Postman opened the
Very Big Parcel. He looked puzzled
when he saw some pieces of wood
and a cushion.

"It's a rocking chair," said Mary
Moore. "We all helped make it. I'll
put it together in a jiffy."

"How lovely!" said the Little
Postman. "Just what I need!"

So Mary Moore quickly fixed together the rocking chair while Granny Green cut the birthday cake and Percy Pringle made a pot of tea.

Then the Little Postman sat down in his chair for a nice, long rest!

Just what I need. I've had SUCH a busy day!